by David Mark Lopez

To Loretta: For taking me to the library

Blue Marker Episode

2

Maddie's Magic Markers

RIDE LIKE AN INDIAN

Maddie's Magic Markers Series
Blue Marker (Two)
Ride Like an Indian
Copyright 2004 by David Mark Lopez
ISBN # 0-9744097-1-5
ISBN # 978-0-9744097-1-9
Library of Congress Control Number: 2003099260

Published by David Mark Lopez
Bonita Springs, FL

Story and Illustrations by David Mark Lopez
Cover Illustration / Book Design by Jeff Thompson
Printed in the United States of America

WHAT KIDS (AND PARENTS) ARE SAYING ABOUT RIDE LIKE AN INDIAN!

You made the book exciting to learn about Egypt instead of a learning book that is boring and hard.

- Audra

I can't wait until you make more sequels. Keep writing and making books.

- Shirley

This is a funny and exciting book filled with all kinds of magical and historical characters.

- Shelly

I usually don't like reading, but this book was a very good one and actually got my attention.

- Kayla

I read your book and I loved it! It was one of the best books I have ever read. I couldn't put it down - I just had to find out if she would ever get home!

- Catherine

I wanted to let you know, John plowed through the book you gave me. He was up at 6:00 this morning to finish it before school.

- John's Mom

Ashton started reading your book yesterday and she can't put it down. She absolutely loves it.

- Ashton's Mom

Maddie's
Magic Markers

Blue Marker (Two)
RIDE LIKE AN INDIAN

by David Mark Lopez

TABLE OF CONTENTS

TABLE OF CONTENTS
(Continued)

CHAPTER 1
St. Louis Blues

The first thing I was dying to do when I returned to Florida was get back to Aida and Caesarion. I read that something bad was about to happen to them and I had to get back to Egypt and warn them. As usual my dad had other plans. The second I walked in the door he was on me like a bad haircut.

"Maggie, for the one millionth, no two millionth, no three millionth time WE HAVE GOT TO GO! We are going to miss the plane."

Of course he knows my name is Maddie, but when he's trying to crack himself up he calls me "Maggie." Now he was pointing at me. He only points when he is really serious.

"Is 'millionth' a word?"

I jumped out of the way before he swatted at me.

I skipped back to my room, finished packing my suitcase and grabbed my pillow and my magic markers. When I got out to the car my dad just shook his head.

"What?"
"We don't have room for all that stuff. I'm pretty sure Grandma and Grandpa have pillows and you are not going to have any time to draw, so just leave

that stuff here. We already have all this junk we have to take for Thing One and Thing Two, so you are going to have to travel light."

(Thing One and Thing Two are what my dad calls my little brother and sister). I could tell he wasn't really in the mood for a long discussion by the way he was jumping around and waving his arms, so I took the stuff back to my room. I did grab the blue marker out of the wooden case, managed to get back to the SUV just in time to see my dad wrestling with the stroller (looked like the stroller was winning) and hopped into the vehicle.

Just for a little background in case you missed my last adventure: my name is Maddie, not Maggie, and I live in Georgia with my mom and Florida with my dad and I am in the fifth grade, and a few weeks ago for my tenth birthday my dad got me some magic markers that really did turn out to be magic when I finally got the cap off and I went back in time to Egypt and had this really cool trip with crocodiles and cobras and buried treasure and now I'm trying to get back to help my friends Aida and Cleopatra, but my dad is pulling my arm really hard through the airport. That was probably a run-on sentence.

"Dad, why are we going to St. Louis, again?"
"Your grandparents are celebrating their 50th wedding anniversary and we are all going and we will have a good time. Did you bring your poem?"
"Yes."
"Do you have it memorized?"
"Mostly."

"Do you want to be embarrassed?"
"You're not going to sing are you?"
"If you memorize your poem, I promise I won't sing."
"Deal."

I already had it memorized, "Song of the Wandering Aengus" by William Butler Yeats, but you can have a lot of fun with my dad if you get him going. I thought about asking him again what an "Aengus" was, but then he would take another 45 minutes to explain the meaning of the poem and how this adventurer had a headache and went fishing before dawn and the fish he caught turned into a beautiful girl and then she disappeared and he wandered for years trying to find her. I really didn't want to go through all that again, so I just kept my mouth shut.

When we finally got to my grandparents' house and got settled in, Dad calmed down a little bit and we went over the poem a couple more times until it was perfect.

The next day was the party, so everyone got dressed up and all my aunts and uncles and cousins were there. My grandparents have lots of friends, so it was a really big celebration and my poem went off without a hitch. The really good news is that I got to go on after my cousin Ben who is in college and is in a rock and roll band. Anyway he played "The Lord's Prayer" on an acoustic guitar and no one could really tell what song he was playing. Hello? I mean after that anyone would look good. When I was finished my dad was crying and told me he was really proud of me. By the end of the party everyone was crying.

I decided to ask my grandmother what all the fuss was about. Now my grandmother is this really cool, creative person who makes the most beautiful cakes and sews and bakes and runs her own business even though she is almost 70. She's the best.

"Grandma, why is everyone crying?"
"I guess it's because they are really happy."
"Why do people cry when they are happy?"
"A lot of people in our family cry when they feel powerful emotions. Today is a day when everyone is thinking about all the time we spent together as a family and all the wonderful memories we created together. In our family there's nothing more important than family."

When I looked at her hands I understood. Her fingers were twisted and gnarled from years of cooking and baking and decorating cakes for the people she loved. I gave her a hug and told her I was glad that I was a part of this family. I spent the rest of the party chasing Thing One and Thing Two around the reception hall until Dad yelled at us and told us to stop.

We had one day to do a little sightseeing in St. Louis before we had to leave. I had been to St. Louis before, but only when I was very little, so it was all new to me. I really love to ride roller coasters, so I was hoping we could go to Six Flags but of course that didn't happen. Instead Dad opted for an educational trip to the Gateway

Arch. My dad is always trying to make me learn something instead of just letting me have fun. Thanks for nothing. I could have been screaming my head off on the Batman roller coaster, but instead I ended up staring at this gigantic, silver 630 foot arch.

"Dad, what's the point?"
"It's a symbol."
"Of what?"
"The Gateway Arch is symbol of the expansion of the West."
"West Virginia?"
"No."
"West Indies? West Africa? West Nile Virus?"
"No, no and no."
"Wild, wild west?"
"Sort of. Go to the museum and find out for yourself."

Another thing about my dad is that he is always making me look stuff up or learn things on my own. It really drives me crazy. If you know the answer just tell me. Anyway the museum was actually mildly interesting. It had a lot of stuff about Daniel Boone, Lewis & Clark, steamboats, wagon trains and Indians. I tried to get my dad to buy me this really neat plastic tomahawk, and he said I could buy it if I wanted to spend my own money. What he failed to appreciate is that I had already spent most of my stash on bubble gum at the dollar store. Now if I had wanted to buy a book about how to make a teepee out of buffalo skins he would have bought me that.

Eventually Dad finally coughed up ten bucks and I got the tomahawk. It was really cool with feathers and everything. The lady at the cash register gave me a gold dollar coin with a picture of an Indian on it as change. No way Dad was getting a hold of it. I slipped it in my front pocket.

The only other notable thing about the Arch was the fact that the Mississippi River runs right by it. Evidently it had been raining a lot because the river was swollen and running almost all the way up to the Arch. While we were looking at it, I guess I got a little too close because my foot slipped and I almost fell in. That gave me chills. After my recent adventure on the Nile the last thing I needed was another river.

The next day we said goodbye to Grandma and Grandpa and flew back to Florida. After the major production of getting everyone and everything packed and loaded, along with a lot of yelling and screaming by my dad we were all finally on the plane. Thing One and Thing Two were sound asleep. I tried to sleep too, but I couldn't so I got out my backpack and fished out my CD player. Unfortunately I had neglected to bring any CDs.

"Hey Dad, do you have any music with you?"
"Absolutely. R.E.O. Speedwagon or John Coltrane?"
"I said 'music'."
"Take it or leave it."
"What's an R.E.O. Speedwagon?"
"If you knew what an eight-track was, you wouldn't

have to ask that question."

"What's an eight-track?"

"Exactly."

"All right, I'll take the Coltrane then."

I loaded up the CD and selected the only song I knew, "My Favorite Things." It took awhile but I finally picked out the melody. Guy could play the saxophone.

"Hey, Dad. This is actually kind of good."

"Right. That's called serendipity."

"Sagittarius?"

"Serendipity is an accidental fortunate discovery."

While I was listening I started fumbling through my backpack. That's when I noticed the blue magic marker just sitting there waiting for me. I have to admit with all the excitement of the anniversary I had forgotten about my plan to get back to Egypt and my friends. I got goose bumps thinking about it, but decided then was as good a time as any. I tugged at the cap with all my might and didn't get anywhere. I would have asked my dad for help, but he was already snoring by then. I cranked up the Coltrane, slipped off my shoes and dug my toes into the carpeting of the airplane. When I looked out the window I saw the vast Mississippi winding off in the distance. I barely noticed when the pen cap slid off as easily as my shoes. I remembered that familiar scent like it was yesterday.

I took a deep breath and started to draw a pyramid, but just then we hit a little turbulence, John Coltrane hit a high note, the pen made a long, dark blue meandering line on the page and suddenly I was fading off into another world. This time I know I saw my dad grinning like a monkey.

CHAPTER 2
Grin & Bear It

When I came to, it took me about a second to figure out that I had not made it back to Egypt. The first clue was that it was a little nippy even though the sun was shining. It must have been like about 50 degrees, but when the wind blew it felt much colder. I knew I was in trouble because I only had on my jeans, tennis shoes and a sweatshirt. This was nothing like the hot, dry climate of Egypt.

The next thing I noticed was that I was standing in what looked like the middle of nowhere. I slowly turned around and everywhere I looked there was nothing but flat land with a few bushes and an occasional tree. It reminded me a lot of Payne's Prairie in Gainesville, a place my dad has taken me to too many times on "educational" walks. He said he saw a buffalo once there, but the only thing I ever saw was a river otter and ten thousand mosquitoes. Lots and lots of flat land. The only difference was on Payne's Prairie you can see from one end to the other. Now, I couldn't see anything but the horizon. I didn't know whether I was in Costa Rica or Canada.

At least this time I wasn't so befuddled and afraid. I didn't know when or where I was, but at least I knew what happened. My magic markers had taken me on another adventure. I didn't know how, but I knew for sure that I wasn't on the plane back to Florida anymore.

I decided that the best thing to do was to start walking. Since the sun was directly over my head I had no idea what direction to go. Even if I had known, it probably wouldn't have made a whole lot of difference. I shuffled off in the direction of a tree line in the distance. It had to be at least a couple of miles away. I started to warm up as I walked, so I started feeling pretty good about my situation. I figured I'd walk until I found some people, size up the situation and go from there. I was so proud of myself I even started humming "Beauty School Dropout", from "Grease", one of my all time favorite movies. I love the parts when John Travolta tries to sing. Please.

While I was trucking along I noticed lots of wildflowers, bushes and berries. I decided to pass on the berries since I couldn't really tell what they were. Last thing I needed was to be barfing in the middle of my big adventure. I kept walking, but the tree line didn't seem to be getting much closer. When I sat down for a little break, I discovered what looked like a lot of plums growing on a tree near where I was sitting. I pulled one off, peeled back part of the skin, looked it over and took a bite. Sweet. That's when I noticed the bear.

I'm not sure whether he saw me before I saw him, but it was crystal clear that he was looking straight at me. He was standing up, with one plum in his mouth and another in his massive paw. I thought about not moving, but I was too scared to just sit there.

During the three seconds it took me to get up and start running I thought about everything I knew about bears. Not much. The only bears I had seen were black bears at the Atlanta Zoo and they were behind fences. This bear was brown, not black, at least eight feet tall and I'm guessing about five hundred pounds. There were definitely no fences anywhere. He was hopefully thinking about everything he knew about ten year old time-travelling girls. What else? Bears hibernate and if these were spring wildflowers, big boy was probably just a little bit hungry. It suddenly occurred to me that my life and my adventure were about to be ended by me becoming a grizzly bear wake-up snack.

I probably shouldn't have thrown the plum at Mr. Bear. My original thought was to frighten him, but in retrospect I should have just left quietly. I've got a pretty good arm, so when the plum bounced off his head, he must have stopped thinking about me like something you might find in a zoo for grizzly bears and started thinking about me as lunch.

At any rate, by the time I spun out I heard him let out a ferocious roar that shook the ground and made the hairs on the back of my neck stand straight up. Out of the corner of my wide open eye I saw him drop the plum and hit the ground running.

How fast can bears run? I don't know. What my Uncle Andy always says is, "Sometimes you get the bear, and sometimes the bear gets you." Neither sounded too good at this point. All I wanted was to get away from the bear. I could hear him panting and snorting and I didn't have much of a head start. I tried my old crocodile trick of changing directions, zigzagging through the bushes and trees, trying to wear him out. He kept coming.

I was running so hard my heart was pounding in my head and the adrenaline was pumping through my veins. I never ran so hard for so long in my life, but the bear kept coming and it sounded like he was gaining.

I made the mistake of looking back and trying to change directions at the same time. When I fell down I figured it was all over, but I guess five hundred pound bears have a hard time putting on the brakes. When he went skidding and snarling by me in a cloud of dust, I couldn't help but notice his gigantic teeth and his bad attitude. I scrambled to my feet, but I knew I couldn't last much longer.

Like I said, the trees were few and far between, but there was one with a low branch about fifty feet ahead of me. Can bears climb trees? I was determined to find out; because I knew I couldn't run much further. By the time I got to the tree he was on my tail again and I could feel his hot breath on my neck. I leaped for the branch and he took a swipe at me as he went roaring by. That's how I lost my first tennis shoe. I knew that gigantic, furry, eating machine could reach me from the ground, so I didn't have any time to worry about my shoe. Thank goodness for all those years of gymnastics. I swung up on the branch and started climbing up the tree as fast as I could go.

To my relief the bear seemed to take a break and catch his breath. I guess he figured he could rest up since I wasn't going anywhere soon. He walked around the tree a couple of times, looked at me and licked his lips. He was definitely not cute. If I ever got back to Florida, my teddy bear was history.

I was just starting to catch my breath and plot my next move when things suddenly took a turn for the worse. "Smokey the Bear" wasn't giving up and started climbing up the tree. I have no idea how a humongous beast like that can climb a tree, but he definitely was coming up and getting closer by the second. I carefully started ascending the tree scratching my arms and face on the thick branches. Every few seconds, big boy let out a roar that echoed over Prairietown and started my knees knocking. I looked up and to my horror discovered I was running out of branches. He kept coming.

He was close enough for me to smell his stinky, brown fur. He was swiping and growling, slobbering and snorting. He reached for me with his free paw and I kicked at him with all my might. Not only did this cause me to almost fall out of the tree, I lost my other tennis shoe. The game was almost over. He kept inching closer and I had no where else to go. I closed my eyes.

When I heard the branch crack I opened them just in time to see "El Gordo", with a very surprised look on his face, go tumbling, branch by branch, down to the ground. He broke about half the branches off on the way down, so no way was he coming back up again. When I could breathe, I thought about doing my little fist-pumping victory dance, until I realized that if he couldn't get up, then I couldn't get down.

Bigger problems. The bear, who evidently was not hurt by his fall, was not giving up. He stood up, shook his head, roared and started shaking the tree. He was going to either shake me out of the tree or just push the tree over. Either way I was dead meat. I held on for dear life, but I knew it was just a matter of time before the tree would give. Help!

When I first heard the barking, I thought I was dreaming, and then out of a thicket of bushes I saw the biggest, baddest, blackest dog I have ever seen. Now, I have a dog in Florida named Shoeless Joe Jackson. He is part lab, part golden retriever and part Newfoundland and he weighs one hundred and ten pounds, but he looked like a puppy compared to this monster. This fearless dog charged the bear, snarling and barking and yelping like a madman.

The bear stopped shaking the tree and probably wondered why he ever woke up. He stood up, roared and faced down the dog. The ferocious dog leaped for the bear's throat, but the bear swatted him away with a mighty blow. He got up, shook himself, and gathered for another charge.

"Seaman! No! Seaman, stop!"

I tore my eyes away from the fight below. Through the branches of the tree I could barely make out a man clad in brown leather with what looked like a rifle. A musket? Davy Crockett? Daniel Boone? He kneeled down and I squinted to get a better look.

"Back, Seaman! Back!"

The gunshot exploded, everything was quiet and then the bear stumbled back into the tree. The dog started barking like crazy and the bear was stunned. But not dead. He fell to all fours and charged the man who had fired the shot. The man did not move, stayed in a kneeling position and reloaded his gun. It was taking forever. The bear roared and screamed, and I leaned out of the tree just a little to get a better look. I heard the tree limb snap just as a second shot rang out. I must have hit every single remaining branch on the way down. I landed really, really hard; hit my head on a stupid rock and the last thing I saw was the bear still charging.

CHAPTER 3
Party Girl

Have you ever had a bad dream that was so scary that it woke you up? I came to with a start, because some huge, hairy animal was licking my face. I breathed a sigh of relief when I realized that it was: a) not the bear, and b) I was alive and apparently well, other than a few scratches and a mild headache. I gave the big, black dog a hug and whispered, "thank you," in its shaggy ear.

Two tall men standing next to me were having a heated discussion. They were dressed almost identically, but I recognized one of them as the man who had shot the bear. He had obviously survived. I guessed the bear didn't.

"William, it is simply out of the question."

"I don't see, Merry, that we have any other choice."

"Send her back down the river to Fort Mandan and we can pick her up next spring when we return."

"Merry, you know as well as I do, she will not be safe there. Either she will be sold off into slavery or married to one of those savages. Besides, we simply cannot afford to wait for any of the men to take her and return. We are already behind schedule."

"We do not have room, William, or the supplies or the space to add another person. And, as you well know, this is the most dangerous and difficult part of our mission. We have no idea what trouble awaits. Hardly the place for a little girl."

One of them looked over at me and I pretended I was still unconscious.

"Do you know anything about her, Merry?"
"Only that she nearly got me killed by that grizzly bear."

I was still a little groggy from my fall, so I just could not figure out why one of the men was named, "Mary". Just then a third man came walking up and saluted. He was definitely wearing some kind of military uniform.

"Cap'n Lewis, Cap'n Clark. The bear has been retrieved, skinned and smoked. The canoes and the pirogues are loaded and we are prepared to head upriver."
"Very well, Sergeant Ordway."
"Might I add Cap'n Lewis, you are an excellent marksman to have killed such a beast with only two shots."
"Just dumb luck, Sergeant. If I had not killed him, he surely would have killed me."

As the sergeant walked away my mind was whirring. Then it hit me like a ton of bricks. My rescuer wasn't named "Mary". He was called "Merry," short for Meriwether. As in Meriwether Lewis, as in Thomas Jefferson, as in the Louisiana Purchase and William Clark. Hot digitty dog!

My blue marker had landed me right smack dab in the middle of the Lewis and Clark Expedition.

I hate it when adults are talking about you when you're still in the room, like you're not even there. While I was picking some burrs out of big dog's fur, I decided to pipe up.

"Ahem."
"Ah, you're awake. How are you feeling, my child?"

I rubbed the back of my head and discovered some dried blood and a small lump.

"I think I'm going to be all right. Thank you for saving me from the bear, Mr. Lewis."

Just then the dog gave me a big slobbery lick.

"I see Seaman has taken a liking to you. How is it that you know my name?"
"Just a lucky guess, sir. I really want to go with you and Mr. Clark on your expedition."

Captain Clark let out a laugh.

"The child is precocious."
"I'm afraid that is out of the question. I don't know who you are or how you ended up in the middle of Blackfeet territory, but you simply cannot join our party. This is a military exploration, hardly the place for a young lady. You will have to go back to Fort Mandan. By the way, what is your name?"
"Maddie Tucker."

"Well, since you seem to already know who we are, I won't bother with introductions. Where are you from?"

I said, "Georgia," right off the top of my head. Every once in awhile you get it right even if you're not even trying. Like my dad says, "Even a blind squirrel finds an acorn every now and then."

Captain Lewis' eyes opened in astonishment.

"Did you say, 'Georgia'?"
"Yes, sir."
"What part?"

I guessed Atlanta probably wasn't even around by then, so I just said, "North Georgia".

A big smile spread across his face and he sighed and looked off dreamily in the distance.

"Some of the happiest days of my childhood were spent in North Georgia. I spent many days hunting and fishing in that frontier country. Do you know a colony on the Broad River developed by General John Matthews?"

The excitement in his voice was obvious.

"I'm not sure. It's been a long time since I was there."

That was the truth only it was time forward, not backward. I decided to try and change the subject. The next question was going to be about how I got out there in that tree and he was never going to believe the answer. Probably not a good idea to try and talk some college football or about the Braves, since neither had been invented yet.

"I know I could help you on your expedition."
"You are NOT going on our expedition."

Ok, he was in trouble now. I've had this same conversation with my dad about a million times.

"Why not? I won't take up much room, I don't eat very much and I know how to row a canoe."

All mostly true, except when I canoe dad does most of the rowing.

He raised an eyebrow and I kept yakking.

"I see that the bear hurt your hand there. I hope that's not your writing hand, because if it is you won't be able to keep up with your journal and you won't be able to write back to President Jefferson and you won't become rich and famous."

At this point Captain Clark was laughing. I was on a roll.

"I can read and write and I can help you keep your journal and your notes and your drawings until your hand heals up. I promise you won't have to take care of me or worry about me for one minute. I can help you take care of Seaman. And best of all you won't have to send anyone back with me to Fort Whatever."

I could tell from the silence, he was thinking it over. Just then there was this piercing cry from the teepee I hadn't really noticed until just then. It was the unmistakable cry of a baby. I went with it.

"Oh, yeah. I've got a three - year old sister and a one - year old brother and I know how to feed them, and change them and put them to sleep and take care of them and especially how to keep them from crying."

He didn't need to know I usually charged eight bucks an hour for all that.

Captain Lewis just walked away muttering.

Captain Clark was still laughing.

"I guess that means you're in then."
"I promise I won't be a burden and I won't disappoint you. There is just one more thing, though."
"What's that?"
"What day is it, sir?"

"May 13th, 1805."

The day I became the newest member of the Corps of Discovery.

CHAPTER 4
Indian Giver

That night I slept in a teepee with an Indian girl and a baby on what looked like a bearskin. I hoped it was one of the relatives of that mean old bear who had chased me up the tree. The next morning the baby got us up really early, but the girl took him out by the fire without saying "boo" to me. I was just drifting back off to sleep when somebody yelled,

"Fall out!"

I got dressed and stumbled out of the tent.

Around the campfire sat about two dozen scruffy looking men who looked like something out of a movie. They all had beards and were dressed in leather deerskin or ratty uniforms. Several of them had long rifles by their sides. I didn't see any other females except the Indian girl. Not one single person smiled at me and a couple of them were frowning. This was going to be tougher than I thought.

Captain Clark strode up to the campfire.

"Men, I have an announcement to make. Late yesterday afternoon Captain Lewis rescued this little girl from a bad grizzly. We don't have any choice but to take her with us until we can leave her with some trappers heading downstream. We'll just have to make the best of it and I don't want to hear any complaining about it. She can help out with the baby and she shouldn't eat too much. She'll ride with Charbonneau in his boat. We're leaving in about 15 minutes so finish your vittles and pack up the camp."

I definitely heard some grumbling and was sure most of the men were giving me dirty looks. Captain Clark must have noticed because he shot them a dirty look of his own and that was the end of the grumbling. I tried to eat a little of the so-called breakfast, but it was truly disgusting so I just stood around until it was time to go.

The man who had talked to the Captains last night ambled up to me.

"Howdy little miss. I'm Sergeant Ordway and other than the Capn's I'm in charge of this bunch. If you want to get along and stay out of trouble the best thing you can do is pitch in and make yourself useful. Start loadin' up this gear and act like you got some sense."

He wasn't exactly friendly, but at least he talked to me and I was happy to have something to do. I started carrying the stuff down to the river and tried my best to stay out of the way. In just a few minutes the camp was dismantled and we were ready to head out.

I had never seen the kind of boat that we were getting into. It was like a canoe only longer and flatter. It had a large almost square sail in the middle. Most of the supplies were in the center of the boat while the passengers sat in the front and the back. I ended up sitting in the back with the Indian girl and the baby. There were several canoes as well as another boat like ours. We all set off together.

I did not see either of the Captains and I later noticed they were walking along the shore keeping even with the boats. They had their guns, so I guessed they were looking for some animal to shoot. Since I didn't have much breakfast I was hoping they could kill me a cheeseburger for lunch.

I tried to strike up a conversation with "Pocahontas", but she wasn't talking. After we had been sailing for awhile the baby started crying, so she picked him up out of his cradle and started rocking him. That didn't really work either. I think she was kind of surprised when I offered to take him. I held him tight and sang "Doe, a Deer" softly in his ear. He calmed down and fell back to sleep. All those free hours of babysitting Thing One and Thing Two came in handy. I laid the sleeping baby back in his cradle. The girl smiled at me.

> "What is the baby's name?"
> "He is named Jean Baptiste, but Captain Clark calls him Pomp."
> "Where is his mother?"

She smiled again.

> "I am his mother."

I sat in stunned silence for a couple of minutes. She had to be kidding. She looked liked she was about 15 years old. How could she have a baby?

"How old are you?"

"I am 17 summers passed."

"What is your name?"

"They call me Sacagawea. The man guiding our boat is my husband, Charbonneau."

It took a few seconds to take all this in. I knew a little about Lewis and Clark and their famous voyage, but I had no idea that they made their journey with a teenage Indian girl and a little baby to boot.

"How old is Jean Baptiste?"

"He was born early this year. Captain Lewis helped me deliver him with the help of a rattlesnake."

I wasn't sure I heard her right.

"What?"

Before she could answer I felt a swift breeze and the boat suddenly turned. Things started happening very quickly. Charbonneau tried turning the sail, but he turned it the wrong way and the boat tipped over even further. On the shore I could see Captain Lewis and Captain Clark jumping up and down and waving frantically. They looked exactly like my dad when he's watching a football game. They shot their guns in the air and were yelling like crazy, but they were too far away for us to actually hear what they were saying. It was kind of like when my dad is trying to get me to clean up my room while I'm watching television. I just could not make out what they were saying.

Charbonneau was screaming too and the baby woke up and started crying. I glanced down and realized the boat was filling with water. It was pouring in over the side of the boat because we were tipped so far over. In just a few more seconds we were going to be swamped and would sink. Out of the corner of my eye I saw Captain Lewis tear off his coat and dive into the river. The water kept pouring in. No way was he going to get to us in time. It was complete and total panic.

Another man in our boat who I had barely notice before stood up and pointed his gun at Charbonneau (who was both crying and praying at the same time). Whoa, Nelly.

"Turn the rudder and bring in the sail or I will kill you now! Turn the rudder, man! Turn it!"

Charbonneau suddenly came to his senses and threw his weight into the rudder. With the wind, the boat slowly turned around and the water stopped pouring in. The man with the gun shouted at two others in the front to row and we started moving slowly toward the shore. There was too much water in the boat. Some of our equipment and supplies were starting to float away. We weren't going to make it.

I spun around and looked at Sacagawea to see if she was ok. She was as cool as a cucumber even though everyone else in the boat was going nuts. She calmly put Pomp in one of my hands and a kettle in the other. She told me to hang onto the baby and bail at the same time. I did the best I could. In the meantime she quickly began gathering some of the things that had begun to float away. She worked rapidly and managed to save most of the things that were in the water. She was amazing. If it wasn't for her we might have all drowned.

Several others were bailing now and the boat was slowly approaching the shore. Captain Lewis was standing near the shore dripping wet, knee-deep in the river. He was shaking his head slowly and was definitely not a happy camper.

We finally got to shore and Captain Lewis and Captain Clark hauled us in the rest of the way. All of the rest of the party came to shore and we unloaded our soaked supplies and articles. I figured we were done boating for the day. Captain Lewis confirmed my suspicion when he let Charbonneau have it.

> "You complete idiot! Do you have any idea what we would have done had we lost the boat? Not to mention the journals, maps and instruments. The expedition would have been doomed and we would have had to return for more supplies and another pirogue (so that's what they called it). You are never, ever, ever, to take up the helm again. Do you hear me?"

I felt kind of sorry for Charbonneau when even Seaman started barking at him. He just murmured something, shook his head and shuffled off toward Sacagawea and Jean Baptiste. Captain Lewis wasn't done yet.

> "The only shame here is that you are not actually one of my soldiers or I would have court-martialed you and given you forty lashes on the spot."

Ouch. After we got everything dried out it was too late to head upstream, so we set up camp for the night. I was really hungry and did not complain about dinner – elk, buffalo, deer or muskrat - whatever it was I ate all of it. No one talked to me, but after we ate I helped Sacagawea with Pomp and we had a chance to talk.

> "Sacagawea, you were so brave on the river. We might have drowned if you had not acted so quickly. Thank you."
> "I only did what I had to do to save my son. You were also very brave. What is your name, little girl?"
> "I am Maddie."
> "I have never seen yellow hair like yours. Are you the daughter of the sun?"

I decided not to go with the goddess route like I had in Egypt, so I just told her my hair got lighter in the summer.

We talked for a long time by the campfire and Sacagawea told me the unbelievable story of her life.

She was born a Shoshone or Snake Indian. When she was only twelve her people were camping at the Three Forks River. A raiding party of Hidatsa had attacked them and killed many in their party. Sacagawea and several other women were taken captive. She was taken north to live with the Hidatsa and later a French fur trader named Charbonneau won her and another Shoshone girl in a bet with the warriors who had captured them. Charbonneau made both of them his wives and they met Lewis and Clark last winter at Fort Mandan. That's when she delivered Jean Baptiste

Charbonneau, little Pomp (which in Shoshone means "first born.") She and her husband were brought along on the expedition to translate.

It was an amazing story. She was just a little older than me and she had a husband and a baby. I felt bad when I realized that she was actually just a slave who had been stolen from her people and bought and sold by others. It was one of the saddest stories I had ever heard. No wonder she hadn't been friendlier.

That night when we went back to our teepee I gave her a little hug and she hugged me back. That felt good. Since my clothes had gotten soaked in the river incident, she gave me some of her buckskin clothes, a beaded belt and some beautiful moccasins. Finally, someone with some fashion sense. I felt better right away knowing I wouldn't have to go barefoot anymore. She also gave me a soft but kind of smelly buffalo blanket and let me sleep next to Pomp. I was starting to like my "new family."

CHAPTER 5
Tale of Two Rivers

When I woke up the next morning I was sore from sleeping on the ground again, but I figured I'd better get used to it. It was probably a little tough to haul around a mattress and box springs in the wilderness. After seeing Captain Lewis blow up the day before, I was just trying to keep out his way and out of trouble.

It turned out I was right about one thing. After the boat almost-tipped-over-disaster when some of the journals were nearly lost, the captains decided to keep two separate journals in separate boats just in case anything bad happened. Since Captain Lewis' hand was still healing I got to transcribe his journal for awhile. We got into it a couple of times over his spelling. I thought I was a lousy speller, but he really took the cake. I guess they spelled things a little differently back then. He put "e's" where they didn't belong and kept leaving them out where they did.

I did get to learn a lot more about the expedition and Captain Lewis. Boy, was that guy smart even if he couldn't spell! He was even smarter than my dad thinks he is and that's really hard to do. He knew about history, rivers, hunting, navigation, science, medicine, plants, animals – he could even draw. In his journal I noticed he had sketched scientific pictures of all kinds of plants and animals that he had seen along the way. He told me several months before the expedition President Jefferson had sent him to Philadelphia to be taught by all the great teachers in America.

That must be why he and Captain Clark were always taking side trips to look for new things no one had seen before. I wanted to tell him about all the cool stuff that would be in the future: cars, trains, planes, television, ice cream, pizza, roller coasters, but I figured he would think I was crazy and give me some funky frontier medicine.

"So, Maddie, how are you enjoying the expedition so far?"

"Captain Lewis I'm having a swell time. I have a question for you though."

"Go ahead."

"Where are we now and where exactly are we going?"

"We are on the Missouri River and we are going to follow it all the way to the Rocky Mountains. At that point we are going to get some help from the Shoshone Indians, cross the Rockies in a couple of days, and find the river that will take us to the Pacific Ocean where we will winter."

I gulped and swallowed hard. I tried to remember from my geography class whether that was even possible. I had seen pictures of the Rocky Mountains and they were gigantic. No way could we pass them in that short of time. I decided to put in my two cents worth.

"Sir, if we can't get over the Rockies where are we going to spend the winter?"

"What nonsense, dear girl. According to the Indians we have already met it is only a short distance between the two rivers. Both President Jefferson and I are convinced there is an all water route to the Pacific."

"Oh, boy."

"What was that?"

"Nothing, sir."

I kept my mouth shut, but I knew we could be in real trouble if we got stuck in the Rocky Mountains for the winter.

The next week went by quickly. The days were filled with hard work for everyone. While the Captains went exploring, the men struggled to get the canoes and the pirogues upstream. We passed through some incredible bluffs and because the water was so shallow, some of the time we had to get out into the water and pull the boats with elk-skin ropes. Often they got so wet and rotten they snapped and we had to go back and start all over again. It was really hard work, but the men never complained.

One day when we passed a bend in the river everyone got their first glimpse of the Rocky Mountains. Even though we were still far away it was easy to see they were covered with snow. Captain Lewis had to notice it would not be as easy as he planned to cross them.

One other thing was kind of funny. In the morning the men would stand by the fire and let the smoke blow on them. Then they would take bear grease and cover their bodies with it. I got a big kick out of this until I got bit about a million times by mosquitoes and biting horse flies. After that I never forgot to start my day off without a big old stinky handful of bear grease and a little campfire smoke.

At the end of the day on June 1st 1805, we came around a big bend in the river. Directly ahead of us we could see another big river flowing into the Missouri. I overheard the Captains talking. They seemed to be confused by this new river. According to the Indians the next land mark should have been the great falls at the end of the Missouri. It was too late to explore the other river so we set up camp for the night. That day Captain Lewis and the men shot six elk, two buffalo, two deer and a bear that almost killed Charbonneau. We ate well that night, but I made it a point once again to stay clear of Sacagawea's husband.

The next morning Captain Lewis had me write in his journal, "Which of these rivers was the Missouri?" This turned out to be a very big deal because we didn't have any accurate maps and there was nobody to call for directions. Come to think of it, there weren't any phones either. If we took the wrong fork it would waste a lot of time and could mean disaster for the expedition.

After talking it over, the Captains decided to send men up both rivers to scout each fork. At the end of the day Sergeant Pryor reported that the north fork first went west for ten miles and then turned north. Sergeant Gass returned and said that after six miles the south fork still continued southwest. This evidently was no help because the captains decided to each take a small party up the forks for one and a half days to get more information.

Each party was gone for a few days. Captain Clark's group came back first. Captain Lewis' party was gone several days longer than we expected and everyone was getting worried. When they got back they told how they had almost fallen off a cliff and had been rained on almost the entire time. Sometimes the cliffs were so steep they had to wade back in the river with water up to their chests. We were happy to see them.

That's when the argument started. While the Captains were meeting and trying to decide which river was the true Missouri everyone else in the party decided to chip in with their opinion. Besides the two captains and myself there were thirty-one others in our party including Pomp, Sacagawea and York, Captain Lewis' black servant. The rest of the men were either soldiers selected by Lewis and Clark or trappers recruited to be guides and interpreters.

Here's how it went around the campfire that night:

"I'm tellin' you, I went up the North Fork and I know it's the Missouri. It's too deep not to be. Besides, rabbit brain, it's muddy just like the rest of the Missouri."
"What do you know about it? You come from Kentucky and wouldn't know a canoe from a wagon!"
"We could send Private Shannon to scout it, but he'd probably get lost."

Everybody laughed long and hard at that one.

Evidently Private Shannon was pretty good at losing his way. I found out later it had happened twice – once for over two weeks.

"Why I oughtta take some bear grease and shove it right into your pie hole."
"I been around water all my life and I am absolutely, positively, most assuredly certain that the north fork is the Missouri."
"If you've been around water so much, how come you never take a bath, you smelly ole mule?"
"Here's the truth, men. If we don't take the north fork we are doomed. We will never make it back to Saint Louie and we'll all be scalped by injuns."
"There ain't an injun in the world that could scalp that bald head o' yours."

It didn't take long to figure out that every single person including Sacagawea thought that the north fork was the Missouri and that was the way to go. That didn't keep them from arguing though and pretty soon everybody was talking and hollering and no one could hear what anybody else was saying.

That's when I decided to stand up on a stump and let go my most powerful yell.

"Heeeeeeeeyyyyyyyyyyyyy!"

I've got a pretty loud voice when I really cut loose and most of them had never heard me say anything, so they actually shut up and started staring at me like I had a third eye in the middle of my forehead.

"Don't you think it might be a good idea to find out

what the Captains have to say since they're the ones leading this expedition? I'm pretty sure they will let us know in the morning which way to go."

I heard somebody mutter something about me being a dumb little kid, but most of them must have agreed with me since they clammed up and went to bed.

The next morning the Captains got everyone up and out of their tents. Captain Clark made an announcement.

"After much study and consideration Captain Lewis and I have decided that the south fork is the Missouri and that is the route we will take."

I was waiting for a big argument but it never happened. Though every single one of them disagreed with the decision, the men did not grumble and agreed to follow the Captains. I guess they all knew what I was just finding out. The Captains knew what they were doing.

The Captains decided to divide the party in two with four men going by land with Captain Lewis and the rest of us going by boat with Captain Clark. We buried one of the pirogues along with some axes, guns, powder, food and other supplies to pick up on the way back and to lighten our load. When we paddled off I was sorry to see Captain Lewis go, as the Rocky Mountains loomed ahead of us.

CHAPTER 6
Flashback

I had been with the party a couple of weeks now, so I was starting to get used to the way things were done. In addition to helping out with Pompy (that's what Captain Clark called him) I also helped Sacagawea dig for roots and helped find berries and stuff like that. I tried to make myself useful and fit in as best I could. I wasn't as strong as the men, but I tried to make up for it by working hard and staying out of trouble. Sometimes they even let me row one of the canoes.

One thing I noticed though is that the soldiers and everyone else in the party were always on the lookout for Indians. It didn't matter where we were or what we were doing Indians were in the back of everyone's minds. When we slept at night we always had a guard. I was under specific instructions from the captains to stay close to camp. Whenever we were in the canoes or the pirogue we always had a lookout.

I didn't really get it. The only Indian I had seen was Sacagawea and she was just about as nice and friendly as anyone could be. One time just for fun I sneaked up behind Captain Clark and yelled, "Indian!" He jumped about a foot in the air and grabbed for his gun. After he calmed down he gave me a very stern lecture about how Indians were not something to joke about and how if I couldn't follow orders I didn't really belong on the expedition. He went on and on. Alright, alright – I get it.

The next day I was riding in the pirogue with Sergeant John Ordway. He and I were getting along really swell. He was also keeping a journal, so I knew that he could read and write and once in awhile he'd let me take a look at it. He had nine brothers and sisters, so I think he was used to putting up with a little nonsense. I decided to strike up a conversation with him.

"So what's the big deal about the Indians?"
"What do you mean?"
"Every time we stop or go or eat or we hunt its Indian this and Indian that. What's everyone so uptight about?"
He squinted at me.
"Uptight?"
"You know: worried, concerned, bothered."
"I see. Well for one thing we have no idea if any other white men have ever come this far. We don't know the Indians that live around here and we definitely don't know if they are friendly."
"Friendly?"
"You know – are they going to invite us over for a nice buffalo soup dinner or are they going to cut our throats while we're sleepin' and scalp off our hair."
"Come on Sergeant. That couldn't really happen, could it?"
"Not only could it happen, it almost did."

Now this was a story that I wanted to hear.

"Tell me. Tell me, please."

"Well, one of the things that we're supposed to be doin' on this expedition is to get to know the Indians we run into. We're supposed to let them know that this land now belongs to America and that we want to be pals with them and tradin' partners."

"But I haven't seen any Indians except the one who's in our group."

"Oh, don't you worry, little girlie, we've seen plenty of Indians and not all of them have been friendly. In fact some of those savages have been downright hostile. Just last September we had a bad run-in with the Teton Sioux and we almost didn't survive."

I was dying to hear what happened.

"So, keep going."

"Well, the Captains knew that the Teton Sioux controlled most of the tradin' on the north Missouri, so they were bound and determined to meet up with them and establish trade relations. Sure enough we ran into a few at the end of September. Three teenage boys swam across the river and through sign language we figured out they had a big camp not too far away. We gave them some tobacco and told them to let their chiefs know we were coming for a meetin'."

"Then what?" I started tugging on his sleeve.

"Take it easy and let me tell the story, will ya? The next day some of them stole one of our horses, so we decided to anchor the boat in the middle of the river. We had a keel boat then and we had some big guns on it. About a third of us went ashore to meet the Sioux and the rest stayed on the boat and the pirogues. Everybody was pretty nervous when the Tetons arrived. That morning three chiefs showed up with a bunch of warriors."

"It started off bad from the get-go because none of our interpreters could speak their language, so the Captains just skipped their big Indian speech and went straight into the show."

"What kind of a show? Clowns, ponies, jugglers?"

"If you quit interruptin' me I'll tell ya. Every time we met with Indians the Captains made the same speech, we did a little marchin' around with our flag, Cap'n Lewis shot off his air gun, we showed them a magnifyin' glass and then we gave them the presents."

"Oh boy, I love presents. What did you give them?"

"Medals, military hats, red coats and tobacco. Well, the Teton Chiefs were not at all happy with what they got. So,we took them onto the boat and gave them some whiskey. They started gettin' rowdy, so we tried to take them back to shore. Three warriors grabbed the boat line and one of the chiefs said we could not go on up the river unless we gave him a canoe full of more presents. About this time Cap'n Clark had enough. He pulled out his sword. Cap'n Lewis was still on the boat and he ordered the swivel gun and the blunderbusses loaded."

"A swivel what and a blunderbutt?"

"Blunderbuss! That's a rifle and the swivel gun was the big revolvin' gun we had on the boat."

"What were you doing?"

"I was in the canoe with Captain Clark, but my rifle

was loaded just like everyone else's. When I looked around I saw that every single warrior had his bow and arrow drawn. It was deathly quiet and no one was makin' any moves. The Captains were not backin' down."

"And?"

"Cap'n Clark started sayin' very sternly about how the group was goin' on and how he had enough medicine on his boat to kill twenty Indian nations in one day. I don't know how much the Tetons understood of what the Captain was sayin', but they definitely knew he meant business. While he was goin' on, one of the pirogues went back to the keelboat and got more men. Finally, one of the chiefs took the line away from the warriors and told them to go ashore. Everyone breathed a big sigh of relief. Cap'n Clark tried to shake hands with the chiefs, but they refused."

Sergeant Ordway stood up and stretched.

"So, was that the end of it?"

"Hardly. Even though our first meetin' with the Teton Sioux had gone badly the Captains decided to keep tryin'. The next day our whole camp went to a Sioux village. It was one of the most amazin' things I ever saw. The Tetons had just won a big battle with the Omahas and had killed seventy-five warriors and taken forty-eight women and children as prisoners. That night they had a scalp dance."

"What was that like?"

"They banged on their tambourines and drums and sang around the fire. They were dressed in their most decorated finest. They had the scalps of the warriors they had killed on long sticks. It was pretty darn impressive and we gave them more tobacco and beads. Some of the chiefs came back with us and slept on our boat. It was a very unusual evenin'. The next day one of our interpreters told us that the Omaha prisoners said the Tetons were goin' to rob us and stop the expedition."

"Did you get the heck out of there?"

"No, the Captains decided to act like they did not know what was goin' to happen. They stayed one more day and watched another scalp dance. That night they came back to the boat, but no one slept much. The next mornin' when we were ready to leave there were hundreds of well armed Tetons on the banks. One of the chiefs came on board and asked us to stay one more day. At the same time a couple of warriors grabbed the boat line again. We all knew we were in big trouble."

"The suspense is killing me."

"Killin' you? We all thought we were goin' to end up at another scalp dance – as the scalps. The chief asked for more tobacco and finally Cap'n Lewis blew his top. He ordered the rope untied and the warriors would not let go. Cap'n Clark threw some tobacco on the shore and demanded we be let go. He lit the firin' stick and held it near the swivel gun to show he was not foolin' around. Just like before, no one wanted to be the first to start a fight. Then, Cap'n Lewis threw some more tobacco to the warriors holdin' the line. The chief snatched the line out of their hands and we were finally off."

"Did they follow you?"

"No, but we didn't sleep well again for several nights, because we were so nervous. We couldn't wait to get plenty of miles between us and the Teton Sioux."

"O.K., I get it. The Sioux weren't very nice. So what's the big deal now?"

He was almost shouting.

"The big deal now is that we're goin' into territory no white men have ever seen. We're goin' to need help from the Indians along the way or we'll never make it. If we have any more bad luck with any Indians no one will ever hear from us again and the Corps of Discovery will be a failure. Do you understand? Do you?"

I didn't say anything and after a few minutes he calmed down a little.

"Oh, and there's one more little thing, Maddie."

"What is it?"

"To make it home we've got to go back the same way we came."

He paused.

"Right smack through the middle of Sioux territory."

I swallowed hard and nodded silently. That night when we camped I kept a watchful eye out for any strange movements in the trees. Later I had a restless night of sleep because I kept dreaming I was kidnapped and scalped by the Teton Sioux.

CHAPTER 7
Portage

When I woke up the next morning I still had all of my hair, but I was a lot more cautious from then on out. I finally got my mind off of it when we arrived at the great falls of the Missouri. They were awesome. The only waterfalls I had ever seen were pathetic compared to these. We had been hearing the roaring of the falls from many miles away, but nothing could have prepared me for their strength and beauty.

Captain Lewis rejoined the company and gave us all some bad news. The falls we were all staring at with our mouths wide open weren't the only ones. Actually there was a series of five falls that went on for about twelve miles. We were going to have to portage around. Portage is just a fancy word for picking up your junk and carrying it with you. Oh boy. The Captains had planned on a half day portage. We were going to need a lot more time than that to get around these monsters.

That wasn't the only piece of bad news. Over the last couple of days Sacagawea hadn't been feeling well and on June 16th she was really sick. Get this. Captain Clark's big idea of medical treatment was to cut you open and let you bleed. He called it "bloodletting." I don't know anything about medicine but I knew that wasn't going to work. He was happy to turn the patient over to Captain Lewis.

I pointed out to Captain Lewis that Captain Clark was making things worse and we needed to take her temperature. When I asked him if he had a thermometer he looked at me like he thought I was insane. Anyway Sacagawea was definitely getting worse: she had a high fever, her pulse was low and her fingers and arms were twitching. I had all but taken over watching Pompy, since Charbonneau was basically useless when it came to child care.

The Captains were especially worried about Sacagawea because she was Shoshone and they needed her to interpret. We weren't getting around the falls until Sacagawea got better.

After Captain Lewis examined her he gave her some opium, some Peruvian tree bark (no kidding) and got her some sulphur water to drink because she was so thirsty. You'd be thirsty too, if they drained all your blood out of you. By that evening she was feeling better. She stopped twitching and her fever broke. I guess Captain Lewis was a pretty good doctor after all, even if he didn't know what a thermometer was.

By June 22nd Sacagawea was much better and the portage finally got underway. The men had cut down a tree and built a type of wagon with wooden wheels to haul the really heavy things. The rest of the stuff including the canoes just had to be carried. Most of the way we were going uphill, so this was incredibly hard work.

If that wasn't hard enough the forces of nature were conspiring against us. First – the gnats. A few gnats are just an annoyance. A couple of thousand gnats can really get on your nerves. But ten billion gnats can make your life unbearable. They got in our faces, our eyes, our noses and even our throats. Not exactly tasty. You could brush them away but hundreds more took their place in an instant.

Next the mosquitoes. Every day they seemed to get worse and the bear grease and smoke trick just wasn't working. I think they actually liked it because they just kept coming back for more. I had bites on top of my bites. The only thing you could do was try and keep moving.

The absolute worst problem though was the prickly pears. They were these small, round, green cactus-like things with one inch thorns sticking out all over and they were everywhere. By the end of the day everyone's feet were cut and bleeding and their moccasins were torn to shreds. Every day I wished about ten thousand times that I still had my tennis shoes. My feet and legs were so cut up I got my jeans back out to wear as extra protection.

On top of all that, the weather was terrible. The wind was constantly howling and once it blew so hard the men put a sail on the canoe and the wind pushed the wagon ahead so they were actually sailing on dry land. Even though the wind was blowing it was still very, very hot. When it wasn't hot and dry it rained like crazy. Once it rained so hard the hailstones were as big as tennis balls and we almost drowned in a flash flood. I threw one of those big hail stones at Sergeant Ordway, but he didn't think it was too funny. I'm not even going to mention the bears, snakes, mountain lions and the stampeding buffalo.

This was by far the hardest thing that I ever did and I think the men all felt the same. They said nothing that happened in the expedition so far compared to this terrible time. Because the loads were so heavy and the conditions so rough we could only go forward for a few minutes at a time. Sometimes when we stopped the men conked out instantly in the spot where they fell. I only had a small pack to carry and occasionally the baby, but it was all I could do to keep up. I felt so sorry for the men, because they had so much more weight to pull and carry.

Despite the backbreaking work and the difficulty, the men never complained. They just kept going and going. We even had a little fun on the fourth of July. The portage would only last a couple more days and the Captains let us take a little break in the evening to celebrate Independence Day. It was America's 29th birthday and we had a great feast of beans, buffalo meat and bacon. The only thing missing was a Krispy Kreme doughnut and some pistachio ice cream!

One of the men had a fiddle and we all danced around the fire. The Captains let the men finish off the rest of the whiskey, so everyone was singing and telling jokes. I even cracked a couple myself.

"Question: Have you heard the joke about the bed?

Answer: It hasn't been made up yet."

Since Sacagawea had never really seen a bed I had to go over that one with her a couple of times. It was a great celebration until a thunderstorm sent us all to bed around nine. I never had any problems sleeping during the portage, since I was bone-tired by the end of the day. The only thing that woke me up was Seaman barking at those stupid bears. I couldn't wait for the portage to end. The next day I almost got my wish. After breakfast Captain Clark said he needed to talk to me.

"Maddie, I have some wonderful news for you. We are sending three men back to St. Louis to take back some artifacts, specimens, journals and maps for President Jefferson. Captain Lewis and I have decided you are going to go with them."

I just stared at him.

"You've got to be kidding."
"What?"
"I mean, sir, you've got to be kidding. I've come all this way and now you're sending me back?"
"Yes, we have no idea of how much more difficult things could get. It will be better for all of us if you go back to your home in Georgia. This wild country is no place for a little girl."

I think he could see I was trying really hard not to cry.

"Haven't I helped out with Pompy? Haven't I carried my fair share? Didn't I help Captain Lewis with his journals? Do I eat too much? Do I smell bad?"

Captain Clark just shook his head and laughed.

I was getting desperate.

"What about the Teton Sioux? How are three men and a little girl going to ever get through them and make it to St. Louis?"

He looked surprised.

"How do you know about the Sioux?"
"Sergeant Ordway told me all about them. How they like to scalp little girls and eat them for breakfast."

He didn't answer, but it didn't look like I had changed his mind. It was time to play my best card.

"Captain Clark, can I show you something?"
"Of course."

I dug into my jeans pocket and fished out the gold coin that I would get as change at the gift shop two hundred years from now. The same coin I had looked at over and over and never really understood until just now. I showed it to him and he carefully examined it. He just kept staring at the eagle on one side.

"Flip it over."
"Maddie, the date on this coin is the year 2000."
"Keep looking."

He stared for a few minutes without saying a word.

"Is that who I think it is?"
"Yes, Captain Clark. Even though it doesn't look exactly like them I know the engraving on that coin is Sacagawea with Jean Baptiste on her back."
"How could this be?"

He stammered.

"What...Why?"

I pulled him close to me and whispered.

"Captain Clark I can't explain everything to you because you would never believe me. But I can promise you this: Sacagawea is going to do something really special before your journey is over. And, Captain Clark, I don't want to miss it. Please, please, I'm begging you, don't send me back."

He handed me back the coin and turned and walked away. I don't know if he ever told Captain Lewis about what he had seen, but there was no more talk about sending anyone back to St. Louis.

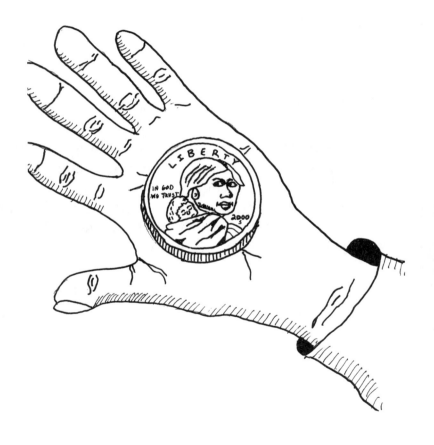

CHAPTER 8
Oh Brother

The good news – the portage was finally over. The bad news – what the Captains had planned to take about a half a day had taken over three weeks. We were still on course, but definitely way behind schedule. Job one was to find the Shoshones and get over the Rocky Mountains before the snow started falling.

Since we couldn't bring a big boat on the portage, the first thing the men did was cut down some trees and carve out a couple of new canoes. When we finally got going everyone was thrilled to get back in the canoes even though we were still rowing against the current. We went a whole week without seeing any Indians and I could tell the Captains were getting worried. Without the Shoshone horses and directions we had no chance of getting over the mountains.

One day when we were paddling along I struck up a conversation with Sacagawea about something that had been on my mind.

"Sacagawea, when we finally meet up with your people what are you going to do?"
"What do you mean?"
"I mean the expedition is going to keep going, right? Are you going to stay with your people or are you going with us?"

She was silent for a minute or two.

"I have thought about this many times. I was only a girl when I was stolen from my people. I don't know if any of my tribe is still around or even alive." "What if they are? What are you going to do?"

Another long pause.

"Even though I am still young, I am a woman now with a baby and a husband. I will go with them. Besides, I want to see the great ocean just like everyone else."

It looked like Sacagawea was along for the adventure just like the rest of us. I knew exactly what she was talking about. Once in awhile I thought about when and how I would be getting back home, but mostly I wanted to finish the trip and make it back to St. Louis. Even when things were at their worst I never wanted to quit.

Just about that time, Sacagawea jumped up and started whooping and hollering. I thought maybe she had swallowed a big bug or something. When she sat back down and the canoe stopped rocking I realized she recognized where we were. She told everyone that she had been on this part of the river when she was a girl. The three forks where she had been kidnapped were straight ahead. Cool. Very cool.

The Captains took turns leading scouting parties on land that went ahead of the canoes to look for the Shoshones. What I could not figure out was why they didn't take Sacagawea. She had been here before, right? She recognized where we were, right? She could interpret for them if they did find the Shoshones, right? Duh. I decided to keep my trap shut, but in my opinion these two guys were ignoring their best shot at finding us some horses.

The Captains never found any Indians, but they found plenty of prickly pears, snakes, gnats and mosquitoes. Every time they came back to camp they looked worse. Finally, a few days later we reached the three forks. It was a beautiful place. Sacagawea told me this was the exact place she had been kidnapped by the Hidatsa five years earlier. That gave me a chill, but she didn't seem too upset about it.

Captain Clark really surprised me that day. All along the way he had been naming all the rivers and interesting stuff we had come upon. He had even named one of the rivers we passed after his girlfriend. When I asked him to tell me about her, he just gave me a dirty look and told me to mind my own business. By the time we got to three forks he had used up every single name in the party and I guess all of his relatives. Anyhow, he told me he was going to name one of the rivers in the three forks after me since I had done such a good job with Pomp and Seaman. Picking all those prickly pears out of Seaman's fur had paid off.

> "So which river do you want me to call, the Maddie?"
> "Actually sir, my real name is Maddisen. Could you name the middle river that?"
> "Absolutely, the Maddisen it is."

I was thrilled when later I looked at his journal and saw he had done just that. He misspelled it Maddison's River, but what else was new? Captain Clark tried to tell me that it was named after James Madison, the secretary of state, but I knew he was just teasing me. You can check for yourself, that river was named after me.

We spent a couple of days at Three Forks. Everyone was either sick or hurt, so we used the time to heal, make some new clothes, and hunt. Well, I didn't actually get to do any hunting, but I picked some berries and ate my fair share. Then we headed back upstream, but the Captains were getting pretty desperate about the Indian thing. Every couple of days they would come back with no news. I could tell they were very worried. The only thing that kept our spirits up was that Sacagawea kept recognizing more and more of the land.

The river was more shallow and soon we would have to abandon the canoes and go on foot. We were almost to the mouth of the Missouri. Finally, on August 17th, 1805 the party left the canoes and set off. Captain Lewis had been gone for several days. When we caught up to him he had at long last found some Shoshones.

I was so excited to actually see Indians I kept crowding up to the front to get a better look. There right in front of my eyes Captain Clark was getting a big hug from what had to be an Indian Chief. Evidently things were going well so far. Charbonneau and Sacagawea were standing right behind the Captains when one of the Shoshone women starting jumping up and down like she had ants in her pants. At first I thought something bad was going to happen and then I realized that the woman recognized Sacagawea.

Can you believe it? The woman had been with Sacagawea five years earlier when she had been kidnapped by the Hidatsa. The next thing you know they were both bawling and talking and hugging. This was really going well. I didn't think we'd have any problem getting the horses and the help we needed.

After things settled down the meeting started again. Sacagawea interpreted for the Captains to the Shoshone chief. I watched her closely when suddenly she stopped talking and got the strangest look on her face. She stared intently at the chief for several seconds. I had no idea what was happening. Out of the blue she jumped up, ran and hugged the chief, threw a blanket over him and started crying again.

You're not going to believe this, because I almost didn't believe it myself. We had come so far, worked so hard and were so desperate. We almost needed a miracle to make it over the mountains and boy did we get one. Sacagawea – the girl who had been stolen, bought and traded like a slave, now a teenage wife and mother, was actually hugging her long lost brother, the Chief of the Shoshones. Her brother! It was an amazing moment that none of us would ever forget.

The Captains were so thrilled with their good luck that they named the place, "Camp Fortunate." They almost got it right. I would have named it, "Camp Serendipity."

CHAPTER 9
A Bitter Pill

Have you ever been so cold your whole body felt like an ice cream sandwich? Have you ever been so tired you could not walk another step? Have you ever been so hungry you would have eaten something really disgusting just so your belly would stop hurting? Stay tuned.

We stayed at Camp Fortunate for a few days to trade for some horses and refill our food supplies even though the Shoshones had very little in that department. They were mostly interested in our guns and ammunition, because they only had bows and arrows for hunting. In fact, we ended up feeding them several times. It turned out they were headed for the buffalo hunting grounds we had just come from to get ready for the long winter ahead.

Since they were going in the opposite direction the only person willing to guide us was an old Shoshone man who had crossed the mountains with some other Indians a long time ago. It didn't sound too promising to me, but we really had no other choices. There was no way on earth the Captains would not keep going.

We finally took off on September 1st and it surprised me that Sacagawea still wanted to go with us. I remembered what she told me before, but I thought she might have changed her mind after spending a few days with her brother and Shoshone family. I was so happy she was coming along. I knew Charbonneau would have not left Pompy behind and that would have left only me to take care of him.

It took me a little while to get used to my horse, but after a couple of days I was riding with the best of them. It definitely beat rowing a canoe. At least that's what I thought at the time.

The Indians called the mountains we were crossing the Bitteroots. The riding was not easy and by the third day it had already started snowing. We met up with some more Indians and traded for some better horses, but the game the men killed for our food was getting more scarce. If we were lucky we found some ripe berries or a couple of birds.

Another problem was that just about every day when we got up some of the horses had wandered off to look for anything to eat. We lost a lot of time finding them and bringing them back. But we just kept going.

September 14th was a terrible day. First it rained, then it hailed, then it snowed. The path we followed was barely a path and was covered with broken trees and boulders. The horses could barely get through and most of them hadn't eaten in days. There was absolutely no grass for them to eat. I spent most of the time thinking about hamburgers, hotdogs, pizza, steak and chicken. I was so hungry I would have eaten anything.

We finally stopped, made camp and the hunters were sent out. I just about cried when they came back empty handed. We were completely exhausted and had nothing left to eat. You may not want to read this part. The Captains decided that the only way we could keep going was to kill one of the ponies for food. I'm not making this up. It wasn't my horse, but it still made me sad. I can't say it was the best food I ever tasted, but I ate it without complaining.

Things got even worse the next morning. Very bad news. Old Toby, the Indian guide, got us lost. To get back on the trail we climbed a very steep ridge covered with fallen logs. The horses did the best they could, but it was so steep we could not ride them and had to lead them by their bridles. Just when I thought it couldn't get any worse a couple of the horses lost their footing and went crashing down the mountain. We never saw them again. The horse carrying Captain Clark's desk slipped and slammed into a tree halfway down the ridge. The horse wasn't hurt, but the desk was smashed to pieces.

When we finally stopped we had gone only twelve miles. Once again there was not one single thing to eat, so we used some snow and the rest of the horse we ate the day before to make soup. It was truly disgusting. No one had much to say that night around the campfire. They were all probably thinking the same thing I was. We were surrounded on all sides by the highest mountains I had ever seen. We had no food. The horses were starving. Our candles were burning low. My new family was in trouble.

When we got up the next morning we discovered that it was snowing. It had been snowing since way before sunrise. It kept up all day. Big, heavy, wet flakes. The snow was so deep we struggled to follow the trail. When we brushed under the trees the pines dumped even more snow on us. I could barely see ten feet in front of me. It was all I could do to keep going. This was really the first time that I wished I was back home. We ate our second pony that night. It was the only thing that kept us going. Before bed I talked to Captain Lewis.

"Captain?"
"Yes, child."
"Are we - are we going to make it?"
"We have to make it."
"What if we don't?"

He shrugged his shoulders.

"There is no point in going back. We will get through these mountains or die trying."

I sat there for a minute, then I smiled. Something just occurred to me. If the expedition never got through the mountains then I wouldn't know who they were. History would be different.

"We'll make it, sir. I know we will."

He smiled at me, nodded and lightly touched me on my face. I slept like a baby that night even though my stomach was empty and I was shivering from the cold.

The next few days were more of the same. We ate the last horse we could spare and Captain Lewis sent Captain

Clark ahead with six hunters to try and scout for food. The only thing we had to eat was some horrible, yellow soup. We kept on going. I had never been more miserable in my whole short life.

Finally, we found a stray horse Captain Clark had killed and left for us and we were able to go on. Things got a little better the next day when we ate some pheasants, a coyote, crawdads and the rest of the horsemeat. Not exactly a cheeseburger and fries, but it almost looked like we might make it.

Sure enough around noon the next day one of the men from Captain Clark's group found us. He gave us some dried fish, roots and some outstanding news. Only seven miles ahead was an Indian village with friendly Indians who had given them food. I thought I was going to pass out with joy.

When we came stumbling out of the Bitteroots we had been in the mountains eleven straight days and traveled one-hundred and sixty long miles. Even though we were more dead than alive, the terrible mountains were finally behind us. We had survived, but we never would have made it without the Captains driving us forward. We were home free. Next stop: the Pacific Ocean.

CHAPTER 10
Rapid Recovery

The tribe Captain Clark found were the Nez Perce. We were the first white people most of them had ever seen. That night and the next day we ate like pigs. Fish, berries, roots - anything they gave us. That turned out to be a huge mistake. Since we hadn't eaten regularly in so long the food made us very sick. Especially the roots.

I hate talking about this part, because it is so completely disgusting. For almost an entire week everyone in the party got sick as dogs. Vomiting, diarrhea, vomiting, diarrhea, then more vomiting and more diarrhea. You get the picture. No one, and I mean no one in our group was healthy. The Captains made it worse by passing out their famous "thunderclap" pills. Those little babies made you feel even sicker. Some of the men could not even get out of bed.

Here's the amazing part. The Nez Perce were so poor they certainly could have used our guns, axes, beads, and cooking pots for trade goods. They would have been the richest Indians in the west. We were all puking our guts out and they could have killed us or just taken our stuff and left at any time. Turns out that another woman saved us.

When I started feeling better I got to talk to a Nez Perce woman who told me a fantastic story.

"What do they call you, my yellow-haired girl?"

"I am Maddie. What is your name?"

"They call me Watkuweis – that means 'Returned from a far country.' When I was younger I was stolen from my tribe by the Blackfeet. I was taken to Canada and sold to a white trader. Many years later I returned to my people. The white people treated me with great kindness and helped me find my way back."

"Thank you for helping us."

"I have told my tribe to repay the kindness that your people first showed to me. You remind me so much of a little girl who lived with the traders."

She gave me a little hug and handed me a present.

I just stared at the moccasins in my hands. The deerskin was soft as velvet and finely stitched with tricolor rawhide. The sides and top were intricately decorated with delicate beadwork. There were several of the large, blue beads the Indians prized so highly. They were so beautiful I couldn't think of anything to say. The several pair of moccasins I had worn out on the trip were nothing compared to these.

"Thank you."

I whispered in her ear.

"I'll never wear them. I will keep them forever to remember you and your people."

I took great care never to wear them and always kept

them close and safe.

We stayed with the Nez Perce for two weeks. The first week we were busy puking and the next week we made canoes. The Indians taught Captain Clark how to burn them out and by the time we finished we had five brand new canoes to carry us down the river. The Nez Perce agreed to keep our horses until we got back and finally on October 6th we shoved off. It was nice going downstream for a change. Captain Lewis was still sick and I saw him barf a couple of times over the side of the canoe. Nice.

The next few weeks we made good time and saw tons of Indians. Two of the Nez Perce chiefs went ahead of us and let all of them know we were friendly. It also helped once again to have Sacagawea with us. I guess the Indians figured if we had an Indian with us we were o.k.

We stopped from time to time and the Captains made their boring Indian speech, passed out presents and put on their little show. I was pretty sick of it after seeing it over and over, but the Indians just ate it up. I wondered if we were going to have enough presents to make it to the ocean and back.

The Indians were all fascinated with Seaman and York. They must never have seen a dog that big and even if they had seen white men they definitely had never seen a black man.

York looked like a professional football player. He was huge and had muscles on top of his muscles. In spite of his imposing appearance he was gentle as a lamb.

He loved all the attention the Indians gave him and even let them run their hands through his curly hair. He was one of my favorites, too. Like me, he loved practical jokes and he always cracked us up with his jokes and imitations. Once in awhile when he wasn't too tired he even let me ride on his shoulders.

Everything was going great. We were making good time and the whole party was in a happy mood. We all knew it wouldn't be long until we made it to the ocean. Everyone was finally healthy and we had plenty to eat.

The river was full of salmon so that's what I usually ate. No roots, please. The men, on the other hand, refused to eat the fish and demanded meat. The Captains didn't want to waste any time sending the hunters out for food, so they bought dogs from the Indians for the men to eat. Dogs. You heard me right. I had eaten some incredibly disgusting food on this trip, but I absolutely refused to chow down on man's best friend. Thanks, but no thanks.

The biggest problem we had was the rapids. As we got further and further downstream they got more and more difficult. Once in a while we got out and portaged, but usually we just held our breath and ran them. Since I knew how to swim I almost never had to portage. One time Old Toby got so scared he refused to go on, got out of the canoe and started walking back up the bank. We never saw him again. I just thought it was a blast.

We finally came to some rapids that we could not pass. The water was churning and splashing everywhere you looked. This was basically your roaring falls with some big old rocks thrown in for fun. The Captains ordered everybody out of the canoes. Then they figured out that it would be impossible to portage our big canoes over the cliffs. They sent the men who couldn't swim and our most important papers around the falls. The rest of us stayed in the canoes.

Now, I've been to every theme park in Florida and have been on some fun water rides, but these falls made them look like a kiddie pool! The natives lined up on both shores above and below the falls to see if the crazy white people were going to drown. Actually, they were probably hoping we would so they could have all of our stuff. We shoved off and I closed my eyes. A life jacket would have been nice. I could hear the hundreds of Indians clapping and whooping it up. Then we were airborne.

When we hit the water again we were going straight down. I opened my eyes again just in time to see us bobbing up and down right-side up and very much alive. I let out a big "woo-hoo" and we just glided right by all those Indians with their mouths wide open. We got to repeat this thrill show several more times before we camped. The canoes had to be repaired a little but we were all safe and sound.

As we descended further down the rivers to the ocean everything changed. The Nez Perce Chiefs left us and returned home because we were now in Chinook territory and they were the enemies of the Nez Perce. The banks were once again lined with evergreen trees and there were birds everywhere. The weather went from very dry to very wet and it rained every day.

Sometimes there was so much fog we could not see well enough to paddle until the afternoon.

There were lots of Indians. They were friendly enough, but they had traded with white men before and they drove hard bargains. We had several problems with them stealing our supplies. It was all the Captains could do to keep the men from shooting the ones they caught.

Even with our little problems we were making great time. Almost thirty miles a day. Then it finally happened one afternoon in early November. The fog lifted and one of the men in the lead canoes started yelling his head off. We had finally reached the Pacific Ocean.

I glanced around at our party. We didn't look like much. Our clothes were tattered and we were mostly skin and bones with long beards and matted hair. We were almost out of supplies and trade goods and had no prospects for the winter ahead. But on that day, at that moment none of that mattered. We had made it!

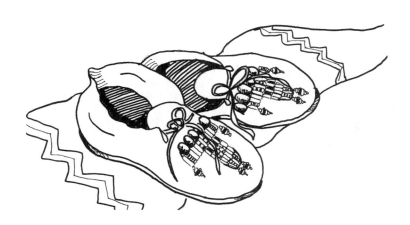

CHAPTER 11
Fort Ketchup

The kitchen smelled so good. There were fresh yeast rolls baking, and the steaming turkey had just come out of the oven. The table was set with mashed potatoes, stuffing, gravy, and sweet potato casserole swimming in brown sugar and coconut. There were pumpkin and pecan pies smothered with whipped cream. I just couldn't wait to dive in and stuff myself full of all that delicious food. Then I woke up. Ugh. Another boring day at Fort Ketchup was about to begin.

The first few days we spent near the Pacific Ocean and waited for a ship to come. The Captains wanted to replenish our supplies and send their journals to President Jefferson by boat. No ships ever came.

It didn't take us long to figure out we weren't going anywhere until the spring. The Captains let us vote on where we wanted to camp so everyone picked the south side of the river, a few miles in from the ocean. Even I got to vote, but it didn't matter since no one wanted to go back upriver until the spring anyway.

I wasn't keeping a journal like the Captains and a few others, but here's what my diary would have looked like every day from December until the end of March:

1. Today it rained.

2. Ate some boiled elk.

3. Bit by fleas.

4. Made moccasins.

5. Have a cold.

That was basically my life at Fort Ketchup. Actually the real name was Fort Clatsop for the local Indians, but I called it Fort Ketchup because I spent most of my time thinking about all the really good food I was missing. All of that food involved ketchup: cheeseburgers, corn dogs, tater tots, French fries, etc. I was even more than ready to eat fruit and vegetables. Aside from the occasional berries the hunters brought back we mostly had elk and fish. Elk and fish. More elk and fish.

The first month we spent building the fort. The men built a smokehouse and then a few huts. I shared a room with Charbonneau, Sacagawea and Pompy. He was almost one, definitely crawling and would be walking soon. He made me really miss Thing One and Thing Two.

Christmas came and went without much celebration. Sacagawea gave me a belt she had made from elk skin and the few beads she had left. I gave her and Pompy some moccasins. The only other fun I had that day was teaching the men how to sing, "Rudolph the Red-Nosed Reindeer."

It wasn't easy. First I had to tell them what a reindeer was and then they wanted to know what they tasted like. Elk? Got me. Then they wanted to know all about Santa Claus and what games reindeer played and on and on.

It got pretty complicated, so I finally just had them say, "like George Washington," at the end. At least most of them knew who he was.

After that it was just one rainy, boring day after another. All of the men were homesick, since they didn't have much to do. I spent a lot of time thinking about when and how I was going to get home. Nothing looked promising in this dreary weather.

Finally something exciting happened. Some of the men had been assigned by the Captains to make salt for our return trip. The salt was made near the sea. One day one of the men reported that a whale had washed up on the beach a few miles down shore. Captain Clark started to leave camp with a few of the men. Sacagawea put up this big stink about not getting to go, since she had come this far and had not even seen the ocean yet. The Captains gave in and I got to tag along too.

When we got to the whale it had already been stripped of all its meat and blubber by the Indians. The skeleton was pretty impressive though and the scenery was beautiful. The Captain bought some blubber and whale oil from the Indians and we left. It wasn't really all that exciting, but I was thrilled to be out of camp for awhile. That night when we got back we had some whale blubber for dinner. It actually tasted better than it sounds and was at least something different than elk.

Most of the time we made clothes and moccasins for our return trip. The Clatsop and Chinook Indians came to visit and trade on a regular basis. By the time we left, we had almost nothing more to trade. All of the beads, knives, axes, hats, ribbons and other trade goods were gone. The men had even started trading the buttons left over from their uniforms. The Indians always drove a hard bargain and sometimes they even stole from us. The men were under strict orders not to let any Indians stay inside the fort at night. I kept a close eye on my coin and the moccasins given to me by the Nez Perce woman.

Captain Lewis and Captain Clark stayed busy writing. Captain Clark made a detailed map of our journey to the Pacific Ocean. Captain Lewis was always scribbling and drawing in his journal. Every day he sketched pictures of the birds, plants and animals he found. One afternoon I decided to ask him about the President.

"Sir, how well do you know President Jefferson?"
"I know him very well. He is like a father to me."
"Really?"
"Yes, for two years prior to the start of this expedition I was the President's Secretary in Washington. I saw him almost every day."
"What is he like, sir?"
"He is a man who has a great passion for knowledge and understanding. Did you know it was his idea to have Congress fund this expedition? Without him there would be no Corps of Discovery."

He went on.

"Every day we would discuss history, botany or geography or some other fascinating subject. While I was with the President, I met every important person in our country and learned from the most knowledgeable teachers in America. It was a privilege to share that time with the President. I am greatly looking forward to telling him all about the wonderful things we have found."

"Did you ever discuss time travel with him?"

"Time travel? What do you mean?"

"You know, going backwards or forwards in time to different places."

"That is impossible."

"How do you know?"

"That's easy. No one from the future has ever come to visit us."

I decided to change the subject before I got myself in trouble.

"Do you think he will be disappointed there is no all water route to the Pacific?"

He paused for a moment to think.

"He surely will be saddened by this discovery, as I was. But he will be happy to know the truth."

It was easy to see how much Captain Lewis admired President Jefferson. I wondered if I would ever get the chance to meet him. I hoped so.

Our time at Fort Clatsop was finally over. On March 23rd, 1806 we started our trip back to civilization. The bad news is that once again we were rowing upstream and most of our supplies were running low. The Captains knew though if they could make it back to where we buried our hidden things, we would be all right.

The thought of all those waterfalls we would have to portage around was also very gloomy. Then after the falls, we had to go back over the Bitteroot Mountains before things got any easier. It was going to be a long, hard struggle, but at least we knew the way.

On the night of April 11th I was so tired I went to bed right after we ate. All that rowing had worn me out. I was just about to fall sound asleep when Sacagawea shook me really hard.

"Maddie, Maddie, wake up, wake up!"

I sat up on one elbow and rubbed my eyes.

"What's the matter? What's going on?"

Just as she was scampering out of the tent I heard her say,

"They've stolen Seaman!"

THOMAS
JEFFERSON

CHAPTER 12
Back to the Future

"Who…,what…where?"

I was so foggy with sleep I just grabbed the closest thing and threw it on. I couldn't find my stupid moccasins, so I had to put on the pair I kept under my buffalo blanket – the pair Watkuweis gave me. When I finally stumbled out of the teepee I caught a glimpse of Sacagawea scrambling up the bank. Naturally it was raining.

I clawed my way up the muddy bank and screamed at Sacagawea ahead in the dark.

"What did you say?"

She turned and shouted as she was running away from me,

"Indians stole Seaman."

My heart was pounding in time with my feet hitting the wet ground. Ahead of Sacagawea I could barely make out Captain Clark and what had to be York. No one else was that huge. Captain Lewis had to be up there somewhere. I kept running but I wasn't catching up. We ran so far my chest was hurting and it felt like my heart was on fire. It rained harder. All I could think about was the time Seaman and Captain Lewis saved me from the bear. I kept running.

When I broke through the clearing I nearly knocked over Sergeant Ordway, but he hardly seemed to notice. About fifty feet away from us stood three fierce looking Indian warriors. Two of them were already mounted on their horses and the third one holding the rope around Seaman's neck was about to jump on his. All three of them had rifles and a spare horse. Seaman was panting so hard I could hear him over the rain. His tongue hung halfway down to the ground.

I had never seen these Indians before. Each of them had long, black hair, wore buckskin and feathers and they looked like they meant business. My mind began to race: Hidatsa? Blackfeet? Could this be the Teton Sioux? The sound of Captain Lewis' voice broke the silence.

"Indian, that is my dog. Release him."

That's when I noticed Captain Lewis standing just a few feet from me. I had never heard that tone of voice from Captain Lewis. He was clearly furious and trying desperately to control himself. I have no idea if the Indians understood what he was saying, but they surely knew what he meant when he raised his rifle.

"Indian, you will not steal my dog."

He paused.

"I will bury this musket ball in your chest."

He paused again.

"I will burn down your village."

I was shocked by his tone. I had never heard him speak to any Indian with such force. Still the Indian showed no fear. He did not let go of the rope around Seaman's neck. He put back his head and laughed. Behind us the thunder rolled. Captain Lewis cocked his rifle.

"Wait!"

Hey, that was my voice. I have no idea why I did what I did next. I guess I knew we had come this far without killing any Indians and without any Indians killing us. I didn't want to see anyone die. I stepped toward Captain Clark and gently pushed his rifle upward.

"Wait."

I slowly walked toward the Indian. I think he could see that I was crying and that I didn't have any weapons. I dug into my jeans pocket – so that's what I had on – and slowly pulled out the gold coin with Sacagawea on it. I carefully handed it to him and knelt down to hug Seaman. He whimpered.

The Indian looked at the coin closely. Then he put it up to his mouth and bit it. He looked at it again. Then he sneered at me and gave me this sneaky grin. He released the rope around Seaman's neck and everyone breathed a sigh of relief. The Indian got up on his horse with my coin. Seaman bounded over to Captain Clark. The Captain put down his rifle, knelt and roughed up Seaman's hair.

It's hard for me to explain what happened next, because I'm not sure exactly how it happened. While we were all standing around, a bolt of lightning struck a tree at the edge of the clearing with a mighty boom and caught it on fire. I was just staring at the tree with my mouth open when one of the warriors scooped me up by the waist and started riding away.

It took me a couple of seconds to find my voice. I screamed as loud as I have ever screamed. The Indian stopped his horse to look back.

I can still see them standing there even today. They are frozen in time in my mind like a photograph I will always carry with me. Rain falls. They are close together side by side, shoulder to shoulder. Captain William Clark is pulling his mighty sword from its scabbard. York is howling at the night sky with his massive fists clenched. Captain Meriwether Lewis has picked up his faithful rifle and is aiming from his kneeling position. Sergeant John Ordway is running toward me, his hunting knife drawn, and Sacagawea is reaching out to me with both hands, her face contorted in a desperate scream. Seaman roars. The wind blows my hair. Distant thunder rumbles. Time stands still.

The Indian turned, wheeled his horse and we rode off into the dark night. I was terrified, but I knew one thing as certain as I knew my own name. This was my family. They would not leave me behind. They would come for me.

We rode all night because the Indians had fresh horses. We only stopped for a little while the next morning. We were definitely headed north. All I could think about is what happened to Sacagawea and Watkuweis. The last thing I wanted to do was marry some fat, stinky, French fur trader. I tried to stop worrying so much and come up with a plan.

The Indians finally stopped to eat and sleep that night. They tied up their horses and built a fire. They tried to give me something to eat, but I refused. I wasn't going to eat their food even if I was starving. Two of them went to sleep and the third one kept watch. I was dead tired, but I stayed awake because I knew my chances to escape were slightly better when only one of them was awake. It was almost morning when the third Indian finally started nodding off. He probably thought a little, white girl had no chance of escaping.

I hoped he was still thinking that when I picked up the biggest rock I could find. I crept around the fire behind him and smashed his head as hard as I could. It didn't knock him out, but it gave me the few seconds I needed for my next move. I ran toward the horses and untied them all. Then I picked the one I thought was the fastest and the freshest. By that time the Indians were awake and scrambling for their guns and their horses.

There were some things about me though they didn't know. They didn't know I had been a member of the Corps of Discovery for almost a whole year. They didn't know I could make a canoe, that I portaged the Great Falls, that I survived the Bitterroot Mountains, that I rode the rapids, that I made my own clothes and moccasins, that I lived with Indians, that I fished like a

Chinook, that I bartered like a Clatsop, that I tracked like a Nez Perce – but most of all they didn't know that I rode like a Shoshone. Who needed a saddle?

I ran beside the horse and when we came to a boulder I jumped up on the rock and then onto the horse. By the time the Indians got their shots off we were flying. We rode south into the cold dawn and toward freedom. I figured I had almost five minutes on them and the best horse. I hoped that was enough.

I did the best I could to cover my trail, but by noon I was in trouble. The Indians were closing in fast. I kept riding south toward the river, but I was exhausted from not sleeping or eating. I was about half way across a large clearing when I looked back and saw them coming. I jammed my heels into my horse's ribs, but he didn't have much left. There was no way I was going to let them catch me again.

Off in the distance I heard the faint sound of a dog barking. Was that smoke on the horizon? It had to be the Captains. Hallelujah! I knew they'd come looking for me. I rode harder. If I could only make it to the campfire.

Suddenly on my left, one of the Indians burst through the brush. They had tricked me. I swerved to the left as he raised his rifle. The barking was getting closer. Was that Captain Clark at the edge of the clearing? I was running out of time. I decided to try a trick I saw one of the Shoshone boys do on his horse.

With my left hand I held onto the simple bridle. With my right hand I gripped the horse's mane. I held on tight and slipped my body over to the right side of the horse. My left leg was wrapped over the horse's back. I knew I couldn't hang on long, but it might keep me from getting shot. Just then a musket ball whistled by.

"Maddie, Maddie, Maddie."

I heard Sergeant Ordway shouting. They had spotted me. I was getting closer. Hang on. Just hang on.

The horse took a sudden turn and I started losing my grip. The sun was shining right in my eyes. It was just at that very moment through my squinting eyes I noticed the blue bead on my left moccasin. Wow: a clear, blue bead full of translucent liquid.

In one motion I let go of the mane and reached for the bead. I was slipping. I tore the bead off the stitching. I had it! My left leg fell off the horse twisting me towards the ground, and the dopey bead popped out of my sweaty fingers. I arched my back, stretched my neck and snapped the bead out of the air just before my head hit the ground.

BANG!

I jumped up with a start and my seatbelt just about cut me in two. My palms were sweating and I was breathing hard.

BANG!

Turbulence. The plane was bouncing all over the place. What was that noise? I turned my head. Dad was snoring like a freight train. I spun around. Thing One and Thing Two were sleeping like babies. My head was spinning. I was back. I closed my eyes and tried to calm down.

"Dad. Dad. Dad. Dad." I shook him. "DAD!"

"What in the sam hill do you want? Can't you see I'm sleeping?"
"Dad, you are not going to believe this, but I just spent a whole year with Lewis and Clark exploring the West."
"Is that right?"

He closed his eyes and went back to sleep.

"Dad. Dad. Dad. Dad. DAAAAAAD!"
"OK, now I'm awake and this better be good."
"Dad, I was part of the Corps of Discovery. I swear. I portaged the Great Falls, crossed the Bitterroots, rode the rapids and made it all the way to the Pacific Ocean. I even got kidnapped by Indians and escaped."

He just stared at me.

"You woke me up to tell me that? Are you sure you weren't in Egypt again?"
"This time I can prove it. I really can."
"Hit me."
"Take a look at this."

I showed him the perfectly drawn picture on my lap of a blue Shoshone brave riding his horse in the mountains.

He just looked at me.

"That is very nice. Now let me go back to sleep."
"No, wait. Look at these."

I held up my feet and showed him the elegant, two hundred year old, Nez Perce moccasins I was wearing.

He laughed.

"Wow, you really got your money's worth at the gift shop. I didn't know you could get such cool stuff for ten bucks."

I argued with him, but he refused to discuss it with me any further so I let him go back to sleep. I couldn't wait to get to a library and read the journals. I hoped they wouldn't leave me out just because I disappeared on them. I put the Coltrane back on and found a squishy peanut butter and jelly sandwich in Thing Two's diaper bag. Nothing ever tasted so good.

THE END

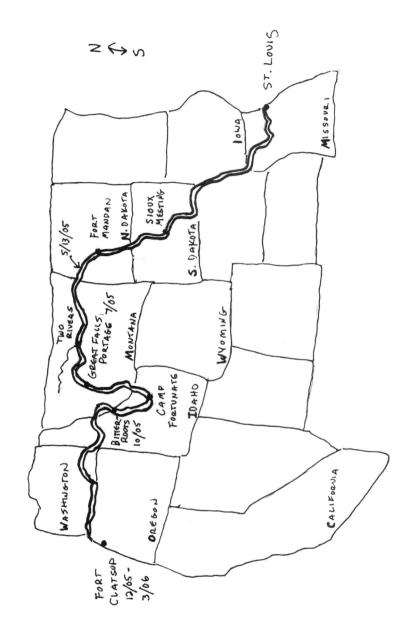

94

Maddie's Magic Markers was written, illustrated and published by its author, David Mark Lopez. Maddie's Magic Markers is intended to be a series of twelve historical adventures. If you have any comments or questions about the books, or have suggestions for Maddie's future travels please contact the author. He can be reached by phone at 239 947 2532, by mail at 3441 Twinberry Court, Bonita Springs, FL 34134 or by e-mail at www.davidmarklopez.com. He would love to know what you think of the books. If you would like to order additional copies of either book, simply fill out the form below and mail it along with your check or money order.

Name: _____

Address: _____

Phone #: _____

E-mail address: _____

Please send me _____ copies of
Walk Like an Egyptian @$6.00 per copy
(includes tax, postage and handling)

Please send me _____ copies of
Ride Like an Indian @$6.00 per copy
(includes tax, postage and handling)

Please send me _____ copies of
Run Like a Fugitive @$6.00 per copy
(includes tax, postage and handling)

Please send me _____ copies of
Fly Like a Witch @$6.00 per copy
(includes tax, postage and handling)

Mail to:
David Mark Lopez
3441 Twinberry Court
Bonita Springs, FL 34134